A Play

The Big Bad Wolf

Story by Dawn McMillan

People in the Play

Reader

Max

Jake

Grandad

Miss Green

Jake's Friend

Reader

One day, Max and his friend Jake met Grandad at the school gate.

Max

Grandad, we are in a play!

Grandad

A play!

Max

Yes! It's *The Three Little Pigs*. I'm the big bad wolf!

Jake
And I'm the third little pig!

Reader
Grandad helped Jake
get into the car.

Grandad *(laughing)*
So, Jake, you are going to trick the wolf!

Jake *(smiling)*
Yes, I am.

Reader

On Saturday, Max called out to Jake.

Max

Come over to my house!
Grandad will help us with the play.

Reader

They read *The Three Little Pigs*
over and over again.
Soon Max and Jake
could say all of the words.
Grandad could say them, too!

Max

The play is on Monday.
Please come and watch it, Grandad.

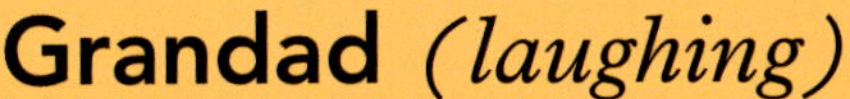

Grandad *(laughing)*

I'll be there. I must see it.

Reader
But on Monday, when Max woke up
he didn't feel at all well.

Max *(in a soft voice)*
I have a sore throat.

Grandad
You have a very bad cold, Max.
You will have to stay in bed.

Max *(in a soft voice)*
Oh, I can't be in the play.
I can't be the wolf, now.

Grandad

I'm sorry, Max.
But you need to stay in bed
until you are better.
I will tell your teacher, Miss Green.

Reader

Max felt sad.
He did want to be in the play.
But then he looked at Grandad.

Max

You could be the wolf.
You can say all the words.
Please, Grandad!
Miss Green would let you.

Reader

So, in the afternoon,
Jake's mum came over
to look after Max.

Grandad went to school
to be the big bad wolf.

Grandad

Little pigs, little pigs,
let me come in.

Jake

No! No! We will not let you in.

Grandad

Then I'll huff and I'll puff
and I'll **blow** your house in!

Reader

Miss Green made a video.
The children loved the play.

Miss Green
Max can watch our play at home.

Jake's Friend
And Jake's mum can watch it, too.

Reader
Max loved watching the video.

Max
I would have been a good wolf.
But you were a **great** wolf, Grandad!